```
JUV         Hopkinson, Deborah.
D
767.92      Pearl Harbor
.H67
1991
0101283547
```

Chicago Public Library
Canaryville Branch
642-46 W 43 St
Chicago Illinois 60609

PEARL HARBOR

PEARL HARBOR

DILLON PRESS
New York

Maxwell Macmillan Canada
Toronto
Maxwell Macmillan International
New York Oxford Singapore Sydney

By Deborah Hopkinson

Photographic Acknowledgments

The photographs are reproduced through the courtesy of The Bishop Museum, The U.S.S. *Arizona* Memorial National Park Service, University of Hawaii Archives (Hawaii War Records Collection), Hawaii State Archives, Werner Stoy (Camera Hawaii, Inc.), Michele Hill, and Andrew Thomas. Cover photograph by Camera Hawaii, Inc.

Library of Congress Cataloging-in-Publication Data
Hopkinson, Deborah.
  Pearl Harbor / Deborah Hopkinson.
    p. cm. — (Places in American history)
  Summary: Describes the Japanese attack on Pearl Harbor in 1941 and its aftermath.
  ISBN 0-87518-475-8
  1. Pearl Harbor (Hawaii), Attack on, 1941—Juvenile literature.
[1. Pearl Harbor (Hawaii), Attack on, 1941.] I. Title.
II. Series.
D767.92.H67 1991
940.54'26—dc20   91-22472

Copyright © 1991 by Dillon Press, Macmillan Publishing Company. All rights reserved. No part of this book may be reproduced or transmitted in any form or by any means, electronic or mechanical, including photocopying, recording, or by any information storage and retrieval system, without permission in writing from the Publisher.

Dillon Press
Macmillan Publishing Company
866 Third Avenue
New York, NY 10022

Maxwell Macmillan Canada, Inc.
1200 Eglinton Avenue East
Suite 200
Don Mills, Ontario M3C 3N1

Macmillan Publishing Company is part of the Maxwell Communication Group of Companies.

First edition
Printed in the United States of America
10 9 8 7 6 5 4 3 2 1

CONTENTS

1. The Surprise Attack: December 7, 1941 7

2. From Tranquil Harbor to Battle Site 18

3. The War Years in Hawaii 33

4. Creating the *Arizona* Memorial 45

5. The *Arizona* Memorial Today 57

Pearl Harbor: A Historical Time Line 69

Visitor Information 70

Index 71

Places in American History

Pearl Harbor

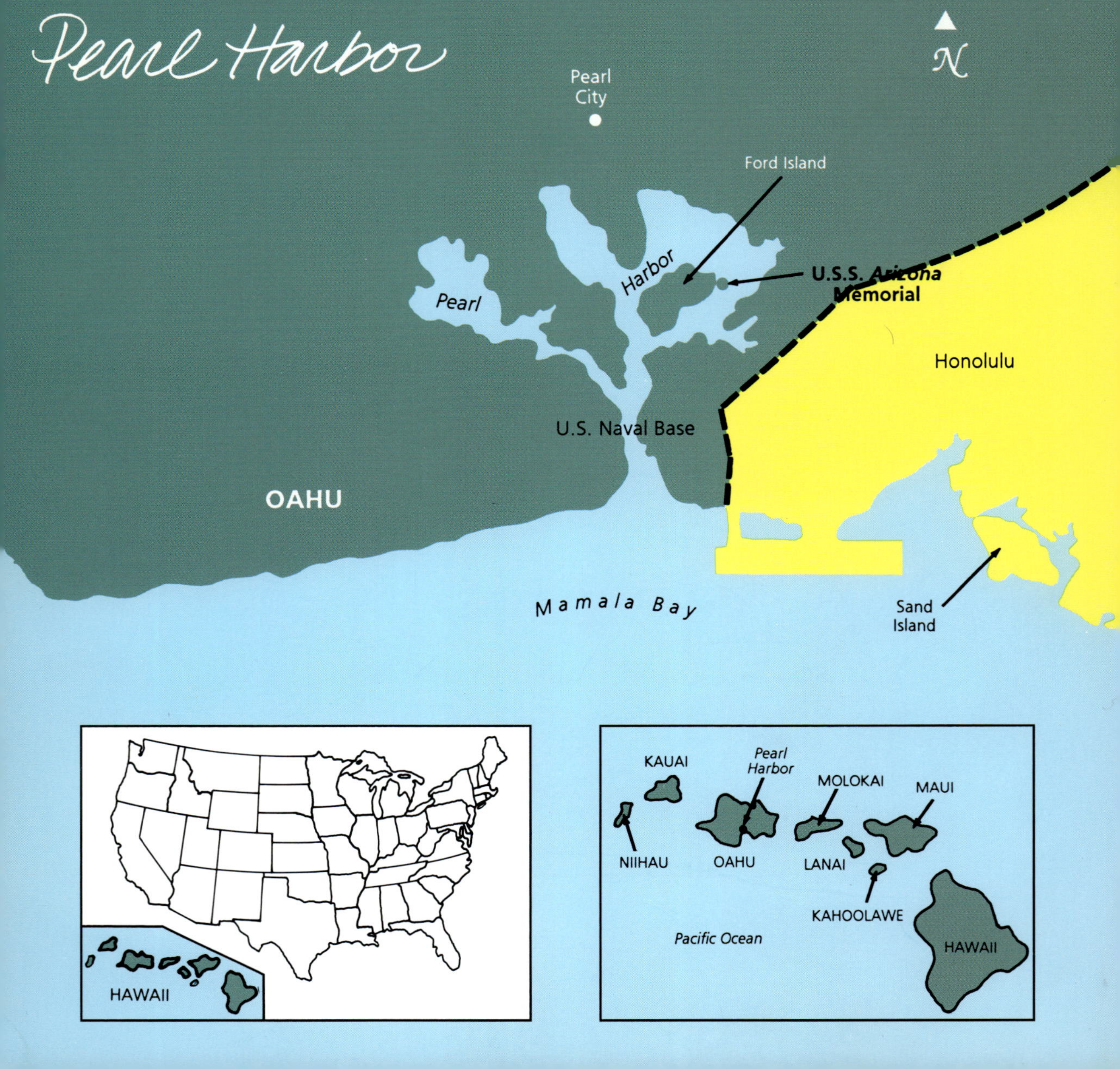

- Pearl City
- Ford Island
- Pearl Harbor
- U.S.S. Arizona Memorial
- U.S. Naval Base
- Honolulu
- OAHU
- Mamala Bay
- Sand Island

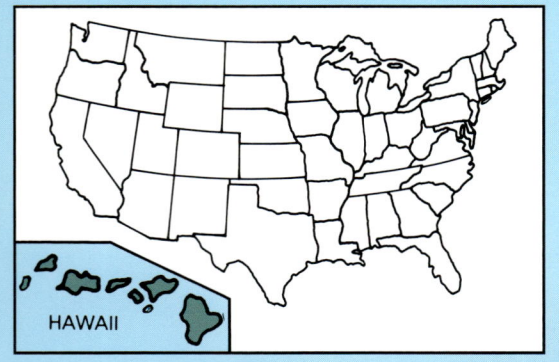

- KAUAI
- NIIHAU
- OAHU
- Pearl Harbor
- MOLOKAI
- LANAI
- MAUI
- KAHOOLAWE
- HAWAII
- Pacific Ocean
- HAWAII

CHAPTER 1

THE SURPRISE ATTACK: DECEMBER 7, 1941

Sunday, December 7, 1941, dawned peacefully in the Hawaiian islands. At the Pearl Harbor naval base, on the island of Oahu, only a few men were on duty. The rest slept soundly in their bunks, the warm waves of the Pacific Ocean gently rocking the boats anchored in Pearl Harbor.

The large, sheltered harbor was home to America's Pacific fleet. In all, ninety-four ships were stationed there. Eight of the nation's greatest battleships, including the U.S.S. *Arizona*, were moored at Ford Island, which was in the center of the harbor. These mighty vessels were among the most powerful in the world.

On this calm morning, America's disagree-

ments with Japan seemed far away. Japan had attacked China and was trying to take over parts of the huge country. The United States didn't think this was right and had broken off relations with the Japanese until they agreed to respect China's borders.

Japan, like Germany, was unwilling to change its aggressive policy. Japan and Germany were allies, or friends. Under the command of Adolf Hitler, Germany had been invading European countries for the past two years.

The United States had watched from the sidelines as the troubles overseas developed. The government didn't want to enter this war and hoped that it could solve the problems with the Japanese.

And then the clock struck 7:50 A.M. Suddenly, hundreds of Japanese bomber and fighter planes appeared in the sky—headed for Pearl Harbor. Their formation was so large that they seemed to cut off the sun as they passed over-

An aerial view of the modern-day Pearl Harbor naval base on Oahu.

head. And then they let loose their bombs.

The U.S.S. *Arizona* was hit almost at once. It exploded into a gigantic ball of fire. Most of the men aboard didn't have a chance. Within minutes the ship had sunk, its crew trapped inside.

"Air raid Pearl Harbor! This is no drill!" broadcast the radio. Heroic men began to fight back as their shipmates lay dying around them. But it was too late.

Nineteen ships and hundreds of aircraft and buildings were damaged or destroyed as thousands of bombs rained down upon the military bases in the area. Worse, 2,403 people were killed, including 68 civilians, or people not in the military. Fully 1,177 of those had been on board the *Arizona,* once the flagship of the United States Navy. Then, just one hour and forty-five minutes after it had begun, the Japanese attack was over. The bomber and fighter planes flew back to their aircraft carriers, which were waiting in the Pacific Ocean.

Destruction to the Pacific fleet and the military bases at Pearl Harbor was enormous. The United States thought it would not be able to stop the Japanese from attacking other Southeast Asian countries. The United States was in for a surprise, though.

The very next day, Monday, December 8, 1941, the United States, under the leadership of President Franklin D. Roosevelt, declared war on Japan. Four days later, Germany and Italy declared war on the United States. The surprise attack did exactly what the Japanese didn't want—it made the United States enter World War II. Japanese admiral Isoroku Yamamoto intended to cripple the U.S. Navy so the Japanese would be able to conquer all of Southeast Asia. He later said, "We awakened a sleeping giant and filled him with a terrible resolve."

Thousands of volunteers, and army, navy, and marine forces flooded into Pearl Harbor. Within a few months, they rebuilt the harbor and repaired many of the buildings, planes, and ships—but not the U.S.S. *Arizona*. Damage to it was total, and it remained sunk in the harbor, its sailors entombed beneath the sea.

Pearl Harbor was the center of training and operations for the war in the Pacific. Hundreds of thousands of lives were lost as battles were played out all over the world. Then, in 1945, the United States and its allies, including France, the Soviet Union, and England, won the war.

People could not forget what had happened at Pearl Harbor, though. Family members of those buried in the U.S.S. *Arizona* visited their loved ones' final resting spot. For the Hawaiians, the ship was a grim reminder that peace could never be taken for granted. The navy wanted to honor the men who had died at Pearl Harbor, too. These people formed an organization called the Pacific War Memorial Commission to build a monument for the troops that had lost their lives in the Pacific.

The U.S.S. Arizona Memorial was built directly above the sunken battleship.

The site they chose was atop the *Arizona* itself, where the greatest single loss of life had taken place. The building appears to rise out of the calm, blue Pacific waters. The long, white structure slopes in the middle, looking a little like a wave. In the center are floor-to-ceiling windows, through which visitors can see the sea and the sky.

The U.S.S. *Arizona* Memorial was dedicated in 1962. Veterans, or people who had fought in the war, Hawaiians who had survived the attack, and government officials spoke at the ceremony. In the years since then, millions of people have visited the U.S.S. *Arizona* Memorial.

Visitors come to honor all those who fought for the United States in the war, and to pay their respects to the sailors entombed in the ship below the monument. They also come to learn more about the surprise attack on Pearl Harbor and how America united to win the war.

On an average day, thousands of people visit the shrine. They stop first at the Visitors' Center, where displays, photographs, and a film tell the story of Pearl Harbor. Guides answer questions and talk about what it was like to live in Hawaii during the war years.

Next, visitors take a shuttle boat to the *Arizona* Memorial, which is in the middle of the harbor. In the Shrine Room, the names of all the

Beautiful views of the sea and sky are visible through the U.S.S. Arizona *Memorial's floor-to-ceiling windows.*

sailors who sacrificed their lives on the *Arizona* are engraved on a wall. Many people cast flowers into the well, which is a hole cut into the floor of the monument. Ocean water sometimes splashes up through the hole. And visitors can see the remains of the *Arizona*—the sailors' final resting place—lying deep beneath the ocean surface.

Pearl Harbor was the only attack on American soil during the war. Strangely enough, the attack was the beginning of the end of the Japanese and German aggressions overseas. It united the American people and made them decide to enter the war—and win it.

The shining white *Arizona* Memorial, with the American flag waving from the mast of the sunken ship, honors the victims of war—and is a monument to the freedom that the United States represents.

An American flag waves from the mast of the sunken U.S.S. Arizona.

CHAPTER 2

From Tranquil Harbor to Battle Site

Hawaii is a chain of more than twenty islands near the middle of the Pacific Ocean. It is the only state in the Union not attached to the mainland of North America. Its nearest U.S. neighbor, California, is 2,397 miles (3,859 kilometers) away.

The Hawaiians make their homes on seven of the biggest islands. They are a multiethnic people, descended from many cultures, including native Hawaiians, Filipinos, Americans, Japanese, and Europeans. There is no one ethnic majority in Hawaii.

The earliest known settlers were the Polynesians. They traveled across the Pacific in canoes more than 1,400 years ago. Many months into

The U.S.S. Arizona.

men to operate it. It was 608 feet (185 meters) long—the length of almost two football fields. The ship had two catapults for launching planes. Its twelve fourteen-inch guns could sink a battleship more than ten miles away. The entire boat was protected by thick armor.

The *Arizona* was stationed at Pearl Harbor in 1940, as war raged across the Atlantic and

Pacific oceans. Japan had begun to build up its military strength and occupied part of China.

In 1940 Japan signed a treaty of alliance, or friendship, with Germany and Italy. Since 1939, Germany had invaded or attacked several countries, including Poland, Denmark, Norway, Belgium, and the Netherlands. Germany's leader, Adolf Hitler, hoped to take over the world. His plans included killing all Jewish people, gypsies, and sick people.

The United States government was against Hitler's actions, but the American people didn't want a war overseas. Meanwhile, Japan continued to prepare to take over countries in Southeast Asia. The Japanese forces needed natural resources such as oil and rubber, which their small country didn't have. The United States refused to sell oil, steel, and other materials of war to Japan until the Japanese changed their policy.

By 1941, relations between the two countries

were so tense that many feared war would break out very soon. Pearl Harbor was placed on alert. Military leaders thought that the Pacific fleet would soon be sailing across the ocean to fight the Japanese.

Then, at 6:00 A.M. on December 7, 1941, an American destroyer spotted and sank a Japanese midget submarine outside the entrance of the harbor. Minutes later another submarine was spotted.

Still, no one suspected the Japanese would attack Pearl Harbor. Hawaii was about 4,000 miles (6,440 kilometers) from Japan—no attack force could get so far without being noticed, people thought.

Then, at 7:02 A.M., an hour after the destroyer sank the Japanese submarine, two Army privates noticed a blip on the radar screen. Radar was a new technology at that time. Radar sends out ultrahigh-frequency radio waves that are reflected from an object, such as an airplane in flight, back to a receiving station. The radar signals would have told the men at Pearl Harbor about the speed, altitude, distance, and direction of any approaching aircraft.

The two privates notified their superior officer, but he thought the blips were American planes. Several planes were due in from California that morning.

But they were Japanese aircraft.

Because of this mistake, there was no warning when more than three hundred fifty Japanese bomber and fighter planes approached Pearl Harbor.

The Japanese commander shouted over the radio, *"Tora, tora, tora!"* (*Tora* means "tiger.") This signaled to the other pilots that the invasion was a surprise and that the bombing should proceed as planned. The attack force had slipped past the Americans' defenses.

At 7:50 A.M. they reached their targets and attacked. Dive bombers rained down bombs on

The opening moments of the attack on Pearl Harbor. Water can be seen rising from the battleship Oklahoma. *Japanese aircraft is visible in the photograph, above Battleship Row.*

the planes parked at Hickam Field, Ford Island, and Wheeler Field. The Japanese wanted to destroy the planes so that the United States could not launch a counterattack by air. Within minutes, more than a hundred planes were destroyed.

At the same time, torpedo planes and horizontal bombers headed for their targets: the

Battleship Row during the attack.

ships on "Battleship Row," where almost half of the U.S. destroyers were moored. If the Japanese could wipe out the Pacific fleet, the United States would have no way to stop them from taking over other countries in Southeast Asia. In fact, attacks on some Southeast Asian countries were already underway!

The vessels were not moving, so they were

easy to hit. Torpedoes and bombs pelted the huge ships. The U.S.S. *West Virginia* sank. The U.S.S. *Oklahoma* capsized in the water after being hit by four torpedoes.

A 1,760-pound bomb pierced the U.S.S. *Arizona's* armor, landing deep inside the ship, where almost two thousand pounds of ammunition were stored. The ship burst into flames. The explosion was so intense that the *Arizona* was lifted out of the water. Then it sank back down to the very bottom of the harbor. Smoke and flames five hundred feet high filled the sky.

Most of the crew inside didn't have a chance to escape. Captain Franklin Van Falkenburgh was one of those trapped inside. Lieutenant Commander Samuel Fuqua took charge of the *Arizona*. But it was too late to do anything but abandon ship. Only a few hundred sailors were able to escape.

It was 8:10 A.M.—twenty minutes after the first attack. Officers and enlisted men tried to

The U.S.S. Arizona burned amidships with its forecastle collapsed.

fight back. But there was so much confusion that it took a while to get the machine guns manned. Generals ran out in their pajamas, awakened from a sound sleep.

In nearby Honolulu, the radio broadcast: "This is the real McCoy! The planes have the rising-sun emblem [the symbol of Japan] on them! It is a real attack!"

The Japanese launched a follow-up attack at 8:50 A.M. This time, the navy, army, and marine forces managed to slow down the attackers. The sailors on the undermanned battleship *Nevada* protected their antiaircraft guns from the heat of the fire with their own bodies. But the *Nevada* was hit just outside the entrance to Pearl Harbor and run was aground.

By 10:00 A.M. the attack was over, but rescue efforts had begun even as the attack went on and would continue day and night until all hope was given up. Navy divers dove into the water, searching the air pockets of the sunken ships, hoping to find some men alive.

Thirty-two survivors were rescued from the *Oklahoma*. The divers had heard them tapping against the ship's walls. After the *Arizona*, the *Oklahoma* suffered the most deaths: 415 of the 1,354 sailors were killed. The total number of dead came to 2,403 army, navy, and marine forces; 960 people were missing and 1,143 were wounded. Nineteen ships, 347 planes, and hundreds of buildings were destroyed or damaged.

In Honolulu, just a few miles away, sixty-eight people were killed and thirty-five injured. Most people were hurt because of stray American antiaircraft shells. The bullets and bombs hit homes and businesses, causing fires throughout the city. The fires burned for days.

It seemed as though the peace of the lush Hawaiian islands had been shattered forever. The people of Hawaii reeled in shock, shame, and rage.

CHAPTER 3

The War Years in Hawaii

"A call for volunteer blood donors! Report immediately to Queen's Hospital!" came Dr. Pinkerton's voice over Hawaii's radio station at 11:00 A.M. on the day of the attack. Blood plasma was needed for the wounded, and if they didn't get it, many would die.

Within half an hour, five hundred people had arrived at the hospital to give blood. The group included maids, business executives, defense workers, and artists. The donors came from many different cultural backgrounds, including Japanese, Filipino, and native Hawaiian. All were united in their determination to help their fellow Americans in any way they could.

Every doctor and nurse was ordered to the emergency first-aid stations to care for the wounded. Trucks and vans were turned into ambulances. The Red Cross served food, and volunteers patrolled the streets as air-raid wardens.

Adults and children alike pitched in to help. Teenage Boy Scouts helped put out large fires on McCully and King streets in Honolulu. Girl Scouts helped out at the first-aid stations and cooked meals for service personnel, volunteers, and those left homeless.

At 11:41 A.M. the governor of Hawaii declared a state of emergency. Blackout orders were announced on the radio and in the streets: "Please turn out your lights....Hawaii is observing a complete blackout....Do not turn [your lights] on again for any purpose whatsoever."

A blackout would make it difficult for enemy planes or boats to target houses or military posts. From 6:00 P.M. to 6:00 A.M., the only lights that could be kept on were those with bulbs that had been painted black. Hawaiians were directed to put black curtains on their windows, too. They readily complied with all instructions. They were afraid that the Japanese would return again.

The Hawaiians lived under these blackout rules and some form of martial law, or rule by the military, for the next three-and-one-half years, until May 1944. Martial law included a curfew, which meant that people had to be in their homes by early evening.

The first night, in almost every darkened home, the adults stayed awake and watched over their sleeping children. They kept their radios on all night, listening for any word from the government.

In the days after the attack, thousands of volunteers united to fortify the islands against another assault. Some built barbed wire fences along the beaches, which would make it difficult

Helping to fortify the islands, children from Hanahauoli Elementary School filled in a slit trench after bomb shelters were constructed.

for an enemy to bring boats ashore. People dug "scare *pukas*," or bomb shelters.

The Boy Scouts painted eight hundred signs for first-aid stations. They collected and dried bags of grass to make mattresses for the first-aid stations, too. Schoolchildren dug trenches around each school. These deep pits would be protection in case of another attack.

All Hawaiians were required to have a gas mask during World War II. These children were fitted with "bunny" gas masks.

Even family pets were put into the service of their country. Nine hundred dogs were used as sentries, or guards, by the military. With their keen sense of smell and hearing, they would be able to alert people if enemy boats were to land.

All public schools were closed. Some were needed as centers for emergency supplies, such as gas masks, which everyone was required to have. Others were turned into hospitals or barracks for soldiers. Teachers were put to work registering all Hawaiian civilians and issuing them ration cards. Without these cards, the Hawaiians would be unable to buy food from stores.

Schools did not reopen until February 8, 1942—and then some classes were held in garages or in homes. Air-raid drills were given several times each month. Throughout the war years, many schools closed during harvest time. So many adults were working for the military that, in many cases, children took their places in the pineapple and sugarcane fields.

Children and adults planted "victory gardens." In all, they grew more than three million pounds of vegetables to help feed themselves and soldiers in the area.

The most important job for the military was to repair what was left of the Pacific fleet. Without the help of the battleships, destroyers, and cruisers, the war in the Pacific could not be won.

More than one thousand divers and repair specialists were flown in to help.

The military's first task was to raise the sunken ships. Five of the battleships were lifted from the water and brought to the dry docks for repair. The *Arizona* was beyond repair, though. And some thought that the fuel that continued to leak from the ship made the area unsafe. Still, workers in special diving suits carefully salvaged parts of the ship and used them to repair other ships.

Two additional dry docks were built. Thanks to the united efforts of volunteers, military workers, and other specialists, some of the ships were ready to sail again within a month. Eventually, eighteen of the nineteen damaged ships would be repaired and see action in the war. But the Pacific fleet would not be up to its full potential for two more years.

Thousands of Hawaiians enlisted in the army, eager to do something for their country.

Since so many men were now in the military, women took over their jobs, becoming, among other things, butchers or mechanics, or running family businesses.

Newly enlisted soldiers were sent to Pearl Harbor from bases all over the country. At the time of the attack, 43,000 soldiers were stationed on Oahu. Six months later there were 135,000 soldiers fortifying Pearl Harbor. The navy increased the number of its forces in Hawaii from 5,800 to 253,000 within two years. During the next four years, the population of Hawaii more than doubled. Most of these people were military workers, shipbuilders, and others involved in the war effort.

It was thought that the large number of military personnel on the island would help thwart another attack. But there was another important reason these troops were stationed on Oahu: It was an excellent training center. Hawaii's climate and geography were very much like the islands in the Pacific where the war was being fought. Troops were taught swimming skills and techniques of jungle warfare that they would soon put to use.

Among the troops was the 442d Infantry Battalion. This group was made up entirely of Americans of Japanese descent. Because of their ancestry, they had to overcome a lot of mistrust and suspicion. Ever since the attack, rumors had spread that the Hawaiians of Japanese ancestry had helped the Japanese. This was not true, and the brave fighting of this battalion helped put an end to these rumors. In fact, the 442d was called "the army's most decorated unit."

But in the early days after the attack, a lot of Americans were afraid that the people of Japanese ancestry in their communities were spies. Despite the Japanese-Americans' declarations of loyalty to the United States, the government decided to put almost all 112,000 of them into hastily built camps called internment centers.

They were not allowed to leave the camps, which were guarded by soldiers. Many lost their businesses, and some were held for the entire duration of the war. Some of the soldiers with the 442d Battalion had family members in the camps.

Most of the people of Japanese ancestry in Hawaii were not forced to leave their homes for the camps. They made up more than one-third of the islands' population, about 100,000 people in all. Still, 1,450 were sent to camps, along with 100 Hawaiians of German ancestry. There was no evidence that any of them had worked for the enemy. In the years after the war, two Hawaiians of Japanese ancestry would be elected as U.S. senators—both veterans of the 442d Battalion.

In May 1945, three-and-one-half years after America entered the war, Germany surrendered; but Japan did not. On July 26, the United States, Britain, and China sent a message to the

Japanese: Surrender immediately or suffer the consequences of a new and terrible weapon. The Japanese didn't surrender.

On August 6, 1945, President Truman ordered the atomic bomb to be used for the first time in the history of the world. A plane called *Enola Gay* dropped the bomb on Hiroshima, Japan. The city was destroyed, and more than 160,000 people were killed or injured. Three days later, another bomb was dropped on Nagasaki.

Five days later, on August 14, 1945, the Japanese agreed to surrender. The deadly new weapon had changed the war—and the face of the world forever.

Like people all over the United States, the people of Hawaii celebrated the end of the war. Luaus, or festivals, were held in the street. Civilians showered returning soldiers with colorful leis, or garlands of flowers.

Today the city of Honolulu is sister city to

Hiroshima, Japan. Just as there is a monument to the dead of Pearl Harbor at the U.S.S. *Arizona,* there is also a memorial in Hiroshima to those who died in the atomic bombing. Both memorials honor the victims of war and remind us how important it is to learn to live together in peace.

CHAPTER 4

Creating the Arizona Memorial

The Pearl Harbor attack had united the American people at the beginning of the war. During the war, the words "Remember Pearl Harbor" had been used as a battle cry, and this motto helped to keep the war effort strong.

Although World War II was over, people didn't forget what had happened at Pearl Harbor. The U.S.S. *Arizona* still lay sunk in the sea. On clear days the wreck, thirty-eight feet below the ocean's surface, was visible from the docks above it. Parts of the battleship, now rusted, emerged above the water, a grim reminder of the surprise attack of December 7, 1941.

Almost every ship that entered Pearl Harbor

had to pass by the remains of the *Arizona*. Sailors on these ships saluted and stood in silence as they passed by. The navy attached a flagpole to the ship's flooded hull, and sailors raised and lowered the flag each day.

Sailors weren't the only ones who honored the men of the *Arizona*. Family members of the crew who were entombed in the ship visited and threw flowers across the ocean's surface. Many Hawaiians felt there should be a monument built at Pearl Harbor.

In 1949 a group of people who had fought in the war joined Hawaiian citizens to form the Pacific War Memorial Commission. They began raising money to build a memorial to honor the fallen service personnel. But the monument would cost $500,000—a lot of money.

By 1955 the commission had not been able to raise the funds needed to begin construction of the monument. That year, the navy put up a memorial plaque on Ford Island to honor the sailors, marines, and army troops killed in the Japanese attack.

In 1958 Congress agreed that there should be a monument at Pearl Harbor, but it didn't have money to give to the commission. The commission turned to the American people to raise the needed funds—but most Americans had never even been to Hawaii. Then the commission came up with a brilliant idea: They would broadcast their appeal to the American people on television.

On December 3, 1958, the television show "This Is Your Life" had Lieutenant Commander Fuqua, the commanding officer on the *Arizona* when it sank, tell the story of the "life" of the battleship. He talked about the ship that had proudly patrolled ocean waters, ready to defend all Americans against enemy attack. The program asked the American people to send contributions to support the memorial, as the *Arizona* had supported them.

Within a few weeks, $95,000 was raised from people all over the country. The Hawaiian legislature also provided some funds for the project.

In 1959, the year Hawaii became the fiftieth state of the union, the commission still didn't have enough money. But the group didn't give up. It sent articles to newspapers across the nation, asking for donations.

In Los Angeles, Colonel Tom Parker read the commission's appeal and wanted to help. Parker was the manager of one of the most popular rock-and-roll singers in the country at that time—Elvis Presley. Elvis had served in the military during the Korean War. Parker spoke with Elvis, and the star offered to perform a concert, the proceeds of which would go to the U.S.S. *Arizona* Memorial. The concert, on March 25, 1961, raised nearly $65,000. That same year, President Kennedy signed a bill giving the commission the last $150,000 needed.

Almost twenty-one years after the bombing

A poster advertising Elvis Presley's benefit concert for the U.S.S. Arizona Memorial Fund.

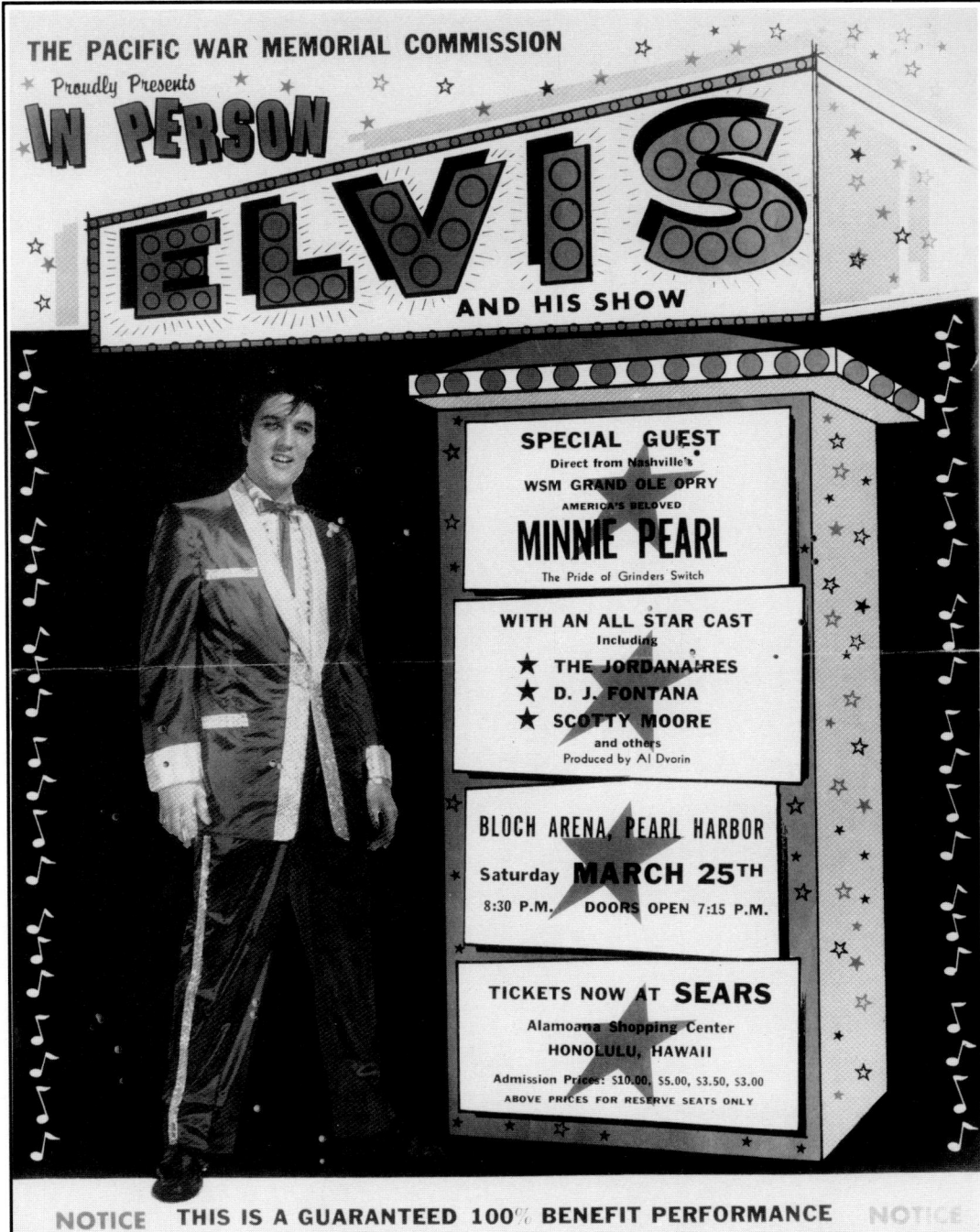

of Pearl Harbor, an architect named Alfred E. Preis was chosen to design the memorial. Preis was from Honolulu and was of Austrian descent. During the war, he had briefly been kept at one of the nation's internment camps. Now he was being given one of the biggest honors of the United States Pacific fleet—a request to design the memorial.

Preis and the commission decided to place the memorial above the U.S.S. *Arizona*. This was no small task, for the battleship lay in the middle of the harbor. Preis would have to take this special consideration into account as he designed the memorial. Its foundation would resemble a suspension bridge.

Carpenters took boats to the site each morning. They drove long, concrete rods called pilings into the ocean floor on either side of the *Arizona*. These would be the support for the structure, which would rest over, but not touch, the ship. The pilings sank ninety feet into the mud of the

Construction of the memorial.

ocean, at which point they were stable enough to build upon. Next, the memorial itself was constructed.

Preis chose white instead of a dark color. With its light hue the monument would give people hope for the future. The remains of the ship, still visible on clear days, would be an ever-present reminder of the tragedy that had taken place.

The memorial was built in the shape of a long, low rectangle. The roof curves down in the middle and is raised at each end, which has reminded some people of a wave. Preis said the dip in the middle represented the low point of the United States after the attack on Pearl Harbor, and the rise on both ends was the nation's high point, when America united to defeat the enemy.

The center of the building is not fully enclosed. Seven windows that run almost from the floor to the ceiling were installed on each side of the building. There are seven more windows on the roof, creating a skylight. This way, visitors are able to see the sky and the ocean. People can feel that, like sailors, they are on the bridge of a ship.

In all, twenty-one windows were installed in

the memorial's center. Some people believe this number was chosen to represent an eternal twenty-one-gun salute to the men who died on the *Arizona*. The twenty-one-gun salute is the highest honor given by the military to its fallen heroes.

The open, airy construction serves another purpose, too. It keeps the building from being too heavy in the middle, where the suspension bridge might not be able to support the concrete structure's weight.

Since the *Arizona* Memorial is about a half mile from land, navy shuttle boats have to take visitors to and from the site.

Construction was finished in 1962, and on Memorial Day of that year, the U.S.S. *Arizona* Memorial was dedicated. Hawaiian citizens, navy personnel, and government officials attended the touching ceremony. Veterans who had survived the December 7 attack gave firsthand accounts of what had happened.

The dedication on Memorial Day, 1962.

The U.S.S. *Arizona* Memorial quickly became one of the most-visited places in Hawaii. In the first full year it was open, 178,000 tourists took shuttle boats out to the site. Over the next several years, millions visited the shrine, and the lines for the shuttle boats became very long.

In 1978 the navy built a Visitors' Center on

The Visitors' Center.

shore, to better serve the people coming to the memorial. At the center, tour guides and a film explain the history of Pearl Harbor and the day of the surprise attack, and a museum displays objects from the war.

In 1980 the National Park Service took over the memorial's operation, while the navy continues to operate the shuttle boats to and from the

Visitors' Center. One of the first things the Park Service did was survey the wreckage of the *Arizona* to make sure that the ruins weren't shifting underwater, which might be dangerous to the memorial.

Divers checked the hull of the sunken ship. Out of respect for the dead sailors, they did not try to enter it. The remains of the 1,177 men were still in their underwater graves, forty years after the war, and would be left there to rest.

During their underwater exploration, divers found one of the *Arizona*'s huge gun turrets perfectly intact. The three giant guns on the turret looked ready to fire. But there had not been enough time.

CHAPTER 5

THE ARIZONA MEMORIAL TODAY

On a warm winter morning in December 1990, a shuttle boat pulled up at the dock in Pearl Harbor. A sailor directed the people standing on the dock to climb into the boat carefully. They were in the center of Pearl Harbor, the headquarters of the navy's Pacific fleet.

These people were not sailors, though. They were tourists, on their way to visit the U.S.S. *Arizona* Memorial in the middle of the lagoon.

Every day, about four thousand people make that same trip to the *Arizona* Memorial. In all, one and a half million people visit the memorial each year—about the same size as the population of Hawaii! They come from all over the world and speak many different languages. So many of the visitors are from Japan that the signs at the memorial are in both English and Japanese. The visitors include school groups and veterans of World War II. For those veterans who were at Pearl Harbor on the day the Japanese attacked, the trip awakens many memories.

Before the visitors take the boat out to the *Arizona* Memorial, they stop at the Visitors' Center. Tall palm trees stand guard on the grassy lawn outside the building.

Seven shoreside displays tell the story of Pearl Harbor. Large photographs show the Japanese planes attacking the harbor. Another display contains photographs of what was happening in Honolulu on the morning of the attack. A Remembrance Exhibit lists the names of everyone who was killed on December 7, 1941.

From the shoreside exhibits, tourists enter the Visitors' Center. Resting against its entrance is one of the *Arizona*'s massive anchors. It

One of the Arizona's anchors—now displayed at the Visitors' Center—weighs nearly 20,000 pounds.

weighs 19,585 pounds and is about 25 feet high. On display inside the Visitors' Center are two four-foot models of the U.S.S. *Arizona* that show the ship before and after the attack.

In the center's museum, visitors see how the tragedy struck home. One display contains several items that used to belong to Paxton Carter, who died on the *Arizona*. Behind a glass case are Carter's high-school graduation picture, his uniform, his last letter home, and the telegram to his family announcing his death.

Large photographs show the entire area that was involved in the attack, detailing each of the military bases and ships that were hit. Another display contains objects from Japanese planes, including a pilot's seat belt.

A theater shows a film about the *Arizona* and the December 7 attack. Rangers or volunteers—some of them survivors of the attack—talk about what it was like to live in Pearl Harbor during that time. Together, the displays and

A model of the memorial and the sunken ship on display at the Visitors' Center.

Visitors board a shuttle boat that will transport them to the memorial.

the film help tell the story of the attack on Pearl Harbor, and of how the American people united afterward to win the war.

Once visitors have viewed the film, they exit out onto a dock and board a shuttle boat to the memorial. From the boat, visitors can see two concrete blocks on either side of the memorial. These are the quays where the *Arizona* and seven other battleships were moored. The *Arizona*'s quays are 608 feet (185 meters) apart, which is how long the Arizona was. All the destroyers are now kept in another area of the harbor.

The first room in the 184-foot (56-meter) memorial is called the Bell Room. A bell from the *Arizona* sits silently in this room. It used to be rung when the captain came aboard and when the watch was changed.

From the Bell Room visitors enter a door which leads into the Assembly Room. Ceremonies that honor the fallen sailors are held here each year on December 7, the anniversary of the attack. In this light-filled, airy room, with a view of the ocean on both sides, many visitors feel as though they are standing on the bridge of a ship.

The last room is the Shrine Room. The names of each of the 1,177 navy and marine personnel who were killed in the attack are listed on a wall made of white marble with

The Assembly Room.

streaks of gray and black. The room is empty except for this wall. It's a quiet place, one for thinking and remembering the dead. There is also a window design of a tree, which symbolizes life.

The memorial also contains a well. Through this hole in the floor, the ocean is visible—and the remains of the *Arizona* lie thirty-eight feet

The Shrine Room.

Gun turret number three.

below the ocean's surface. Fish feed on the plants growing on the wreck. The round, rusting top of gun turret number three sticks up above the water. There is often a rainbow swirl on the water. It's caused by the oil that is still leaking from the *Arizona* after fifty years. People make offerings of flower leis, tossing them into the calm waters of the well. After touring the memorial, many visitors soberly imagine that not-so-peaceful day in 1941.

Historians working at the *Arizona* continue to interpret Pearl Harbor's past to visitors today. The research center of the *Arizona* conducts ongoing interviews with survivors of the attack, both civilian and military. These people's stories are available on tape in the memorial's research center. Additional exhibits honoring those involved in the attack are planned. They will include more objects, letters, and photographs of the war. Starting in 1993, there will be interactive computer programs, too.

Another new exhibit that is now being planned was a bit of a surprise to the workers at the monument—and to the navy. In May 1991, workers were using a dredger to do a routine cleanup of the bottom of Pearl Harbor. When the machine's big shovel was raised, emerging with the mud was an eighteen-foot-long Japanese torpedo from the December 7 attack! And it was still activated, or live, as the navy discovered when it called in its bomb experts and had the torpedo detonated, or exploded. The pieces of the torpedo will be used in one of the *Arizona* Visitors' Center displays.

The workers at the memorial feel it is important to remember and learn from the past so that tragedies like World War II will never happen again. They are planning a special commemoration on December 7, 1991, the fiftieth anniversary of the attack. President Bush is scheduled to speak at the ceremony.

Visiting the U.S.S. *Arizona* Memorial is an opportunity to remember with respect and honor those who sacrificed their lives during the war. The memorial is also a symbol of the need to seek peaceful ways of solving problems between nations. If the people of the world can achieve this, there need not be war anymore. Then, perhaps, future memorials will all be to peace.

Pearl Harbor: A Historical Time Line

1941   Japan bombs the American naval base at Pearl Harbor bringing the U.S. into World War II.

1941–1944   Hawaiians live under blackout rules and martial law; Hawaiians of all ages partake in the war effort and in fortifying their islands against further attack.

1945   President Truman orders an atomic bomb to be dropped on Hiroshima and Nagasaki, Japan; World War II ends.

1949   The Pacific War Memorial Commission is formed to build a memorial to military personnel who died at Pearl Harbor in 1941.

1961   Elvis Presley gives a benefit concert to help raise money for the memorial.

1962   The U.S.S. *Arizona* Memorial is completed and dedicated.

1978   The Visitors' Center is built on shore near the memorial.

1980   The National Park Service takes over the memorial's operation.

1991   A commemoration will take place at the memorial on December 7, the fiftieth anniversary of the attack.

Visitor Information

Hours
Visitors' Center: 7:30 A.M. to 5:00 P.M., every day. Memorial Program: 7:45 A.M. to 3:00 P.M., weather permitting; memorial programs are not available on Thanksgiving, Christmas, and New Year's Day.

Visitors' Center
Visitors may explore museum exhibits, a bookstore, a snack shop; they may see a short film at the theater about the *Arizona* and the Pearl Harbor attack.

Memorial Program
The program lasts about 1 hour and 15 minutes. The program is free, but it is a good idea to plan visits early in the day; programs are filled on a first-come, first-served basis. Children under 11 must have a parent with them to ride the boat to the memorial. Children must be at least 45 inches tall to take the boat ride. At the memorial, visitors have about 20 minutes to look around the Bell Room, Shrine Room, and Assembly Room.

Additional information can be obtained from:
The Superintendent
U.S.S. *Arizona* Memorial
#1 *Arizona* Memorial Place
Honolulu, Hawaii 96818
(808) 422-0561

Index

atomic bomb, 43-44
"Battleship Row," 27-28
blackouts, 34-35
bomb shelters, 36
Boy Scouts, 34, 36
Bush, President George, 68
Carter, Paxton, 60
China, 9, 24, 43
Cook, Captain James, 20, 21
England, 12, 20, 43
Ford Island, 7, 27, 46
442d Infantry Battalion, 41-42
France, 12, 20
Fuqua, Lieutenant Commander Samuel, 29, 47
Germany, 9, 11, 17, 24, 42
Girl Scouts, 34
Hawaii: civilians killed on December 7, 1941 attack at, 32; early history of, 18-21; inhabited islands of, 18; location of, 18; population during World War II of, 40; settlers on, 18-19, 20-21; war efforts of Americans during World War II in, 33-41
Hiroshima, Japan, 43
Hitler, Adolf, 9, 24
Honolulu, Hawaii, 30, 32, 34, 44, 50, 58
Italy, 11, 24
Japan, 9-11, 17, 23-28, 30, 35, 42-44, 58
Japanese-Americans, 41-42
Kamehameha I, King, 20

Nagasaki, Japan, 43
Oahu, 7, 19, 40
Pacific Ocean, 7, 10, 12, 13, 18, 23, 38
Pacific War Memorial Commission, 12, 46-50
Parker, Colonel Tom, 48
Pearl Harbor, Hawaii: early history of, 19-20; naming of, 20
Pearl Harbor naval base: construction of, 22; December 7, 1941 attack on, 7-10, 25-32; destruction of, 10, 11, 29-32; location of, 7; number of ships at, 7; people killed at, 10, 29, 31-32; repair of, 11-12, 28-39; rescue efforts at, 31; shark goddess and, 22
Preis, Alfred E., 50-52
Presley, Elvis, 48
Roosevelt, President Franklin D., 11
Soviet Union, 12
Spain, 20
"This Is Your Life," 47
U.S.S. *Arizona*: ammunition on, 23, 56; bombing of, 10, 29; cost of, 22; men entombed in, 10, 12, 29, 56; number of men who operated, 22; size of, 22-23, 63; survey of wreckage of,

56; visible remains of, 45
U.S.S. *Arizona* Memorial: anchor at, 58-60; Assembly Room at, 63; Bell Room at, 63; construction of, 50-53; dedication of, 15, 53; design of, 13, 50-53, 64; fiftieth anniversary of attack at, 68; fund raising for, 46-48; historians and, 67; Japanese torpedo found at, 67-68; models at, 60; National Park Service and, 55-56; number of tourists at, 15, 54, 57; Remembrance Exhibit at, 58; Shrine Room at, 15-17, 63-64; site of, 13, 50, 53; tours of, 55, 58-67; visible remains of *Arizona* at, 17, 52, 64-66; Visitors' Center at, 15, 54, 58; "wishing well" at, 17, 64, 66
U.S.S. *Nevada*, 31
U.S.S. *Oklahoma*, 29, 31
U.S.S. *West Virginia*, 29

Vancouver, Captain George, 20

"victory gardens," 38

World War II, 11-12, 15, 17, 23, 33-44, 45, 46, 58, 68

Yamamoto, Admiral, 11